I Can Hear!

First published in 2010
by Wayland

This paperback edition published in 2011 by Wayland

Text copyright © Louise John
Illustration copyright © Andy Elkerton

Wayland
338 Euston Road
London NW1 3BH

Wayland Australia
Level 17/207 Kent Street
Sydney, NSW 2000

Series Editor: Louise John
Editor: Katie Powell
Cover design: Paul Cherrill
Design: D.R.ink
Consultant: Shirley Bickler

A CIP catalogue record for this book is available from the British Library.

ISBN 9780750260091 (hbk)
ISBN 9780750260138 (pbk)

Printed in China

Wayland is a division of Hachette Children's Books,
an Hachette UK Company

www.hachette.co.uk

I Can Hear!

Written by Louise John
Illustrated by Andy Elkerton

WAYLAND

Sh! I can hear
the birds singing.

Sh! I can hear

the wind blowing.

Sh! I can hear
the water splashing.

Splash, splash!

9

Sh! I can hear

the children laughing.

Sh! I can hear
Dad shouting.

Sh! I can hear
the baby crying.

Sh! I can hear
the dog barking.

Sh! I can hear
the band playing.

I can hear!

Guiding a First Read of
I Can Hear!

It is important to talk through the book with the child before they read it alone. This prepares them for the way the story unfolds, and allows them to enjoy the pictures as you both talk naturally, using the language they will later encounter when reading. Read them the brief overview below, and then follow the suggestions.

1. Talking through the book
This boy cannot hear well, but he uses a hearing aid so he can listen to lots of different sounds. Can you see his hearing aid?

> Let's read the title: **I Can Hear!**
> Now we'll look at the pictures.
> On page 4, the boy says, "Sh! I can hear the birds singing."
> And the birds say, "Tweet! Tweet!"
> Let's find out what he can hear on the next page.
> He says, "I can hear the wind blowing."

Continue through the book, guiding the discussion to fit the text as the child looks at the illustrations.

> On page 18, what does he say? Yes, "I can hear the band playing." Boom! Boom! And on the last page, he looks happy because he can hear properly.

2. A first reading of the book

Ask the child to read the book independently, pointing carefully under each word (tracking), while thinking about the story. Praise attempts by the child to correct themselves, and prompt them to use their letter knowledge, the punctuation and check the meaning, for example:

You said, "The children are playing".
What does 'playing' begin with?
Now check to see if this word begins with 'p'.
What else could it be? Is 'laughing' right?
Well done.

You said, "The dog is woofing". Then you changed it when you spotted 'b' at the beginning of 'barking.' Good checking.

3. Follow-up activities

The high frequency words in this title are:
can   I   the

- Select a new high frequency word, and ask the child or group to find it throughout the book. Discuss the shape of the letters and the letter sounds.
- To memorise the word, ask the child to write it in the air, then write it repeatedly on a whiteboard or on paper, leaving a space between each attempt.

4. Encourage

- Reading the book again – with expression.
- Drawing a picture based on the story.
- Writing one or two sentences using the practised words.

23

START READING is a series of highly enjoyable books for beginner readers. **The books have been carefully graded to match the Book Bands widely used in schools.** This enables readers to be sure they choose books that match their own reading ability.

Look out for the Band colour on the book in our Start Reading logo.

The Bands are:

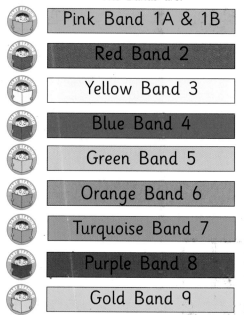

	Pink Band 1A & 1B
	Red Band 2
	Yellow Band 3
	Blue Band 4
	Green Band 5
	Orange Band 6
	Turquoise Band 7
	Purple Band 8
	Gold Band 9

START READING books can be read independently or shared with an adult. They promote the enjoyment of reading through satisfying stories supported by fun illustrations.

Louise John is really the editor of Start Reading, but wanted to see how she liked writing books, too. It was quite tricky, but she found that eating lots of chocolate biscuits made her think better! She tries out her ideas on her daughter, Amelia, who tells her if they are any good or not!

Andy Elkerton spent three years at art college before becoming an artist in the world of computer games. Eventually he escaped and now spends his time illustrating children's books like these.